Butterfly House

BY Eve Bunting
ILLUSTRATED BY Greg Shed

SCHOLASTIC PRESS · NEW YORK

Special thanks to
SHERRY CAISLEY,
KIDSPACE MUSEUM,
and
CAROLYN KLASS,
DEPARTMENT OF ENTOMOLOGY,
CORNELL UNIVERSITY,
for reviewing the
information on how
to raise a butterfly.

Text copyright © 1999 by Edward D. Bunting and Anne E. Bunting Family Trust
Illustrations copyright © 1999 by Greg Shed
All rights reserved. Published by Scholastic Press, a division of Scholastic Inc., Publishers since 1920.
SCHOLASTIC and SCHOLASTIC PRESS and associated logos are trademarks and/or
registered trademarks of Scholastic Inc.

LIBRARY OF CONGRESS CATALOGING-IN-PUBLICATION DATA
Bunting, Eve, 1928-
Butterfly house / by Eve Bunting; illustrated by Greg Shed.   p.   cm.
Summary: With the help of her grandfather, a little girl makes a house for a larva and watches
it develop before setting it free, and every spring after that butterflies come to visit her.
ISBN 0-590-84884-4
[1. Butterflies—Fiction. 2. Metamorphosis—Fiction. 3. Grandfathers—Fiction.
4. Stories in rhyme.] I. Shed, Greg, ill. II. Title.
PZ8.3.B92Bu   1999
[E]—dc21   98-16349   CIP   AC

10 9 8 7 6 5 4 3 2 1   9/9 0/0 01 02 03

Printed in Mexico   49
First edition, May 1999

The text type was set in Joanna.
The display type was set in Snell Roundhand.
The illustrations were rendered in gouache on canvas.
Book design by Marijka Kostiw

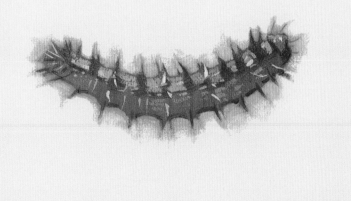

WHEN I WAS JUST A LITTLE GIRL
I saw a small black creature
like a tiny worm,
and saved it from a greedy jay
who wanted it
for lunch.

I carried it inside,
safe on its wide green leaf.
My grandpa said
it was a larva
and soon would be
a butterfly.

We laid the larva carefully
on thistle leaves
inside an empty jar,
put in a twig
for it to climb—
then made a lid
of soft white paper
all stuck around with glue.
My grandpa knew
exactly what to do.
"I raised a butterfly myself," he said,
"when I was just your age."

How strange to think
my grandpa once
was young like me.
"We would have been best friends
if I'd been there back then," I said.
My grandpa smiled.
"It worked out anyhow.
We're best friends now."

Up in his room
we found a box.
I cut a window in its side,
then covered it with screen.
Soon I could look inside and see
my larva
looking back at me.

What would she see?
A human face
so big and scary,
strange and starey?
What would she think?

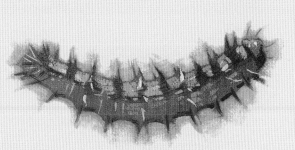

"I want it pretty till she goes," I said.
And so
Grandpa and I drew flowers
on colored paper.
Cone flowers, purple-blue,
and marigolds,
latana, bright as flame,
and thistles, too.

We wedged a garden twig inside the box
for her to walk on,
so her wings could dry
once she became a butterfly.

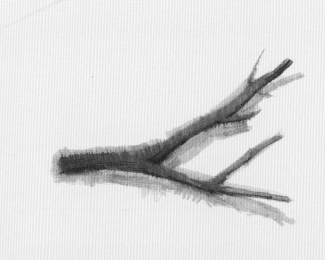

My grandpa knows
the flowers
butterflies like best.
The ones where they can rest
and drink
the sweet, clear nectar.

We glued the painted flowers inside the box
so it was bright with color.
Made a sky above,
the lid all blue
with small white cotton clouds,
and green with tops of trees
that seemed to sway
in soundless air.

I made a curve of rainbow
like a hug
to keep her safe
while she was there.
We set the jar inside and closed the painted lid.
Through the screened window
I could see the garden house.
A place of flowers
and space
and waiting stillness.

Each day I put out leaves for food
and watched my larva change.

My Grandpa knew when it was time
to gently pull away
the paper top she hung from.
I taped it to the wall inside her house
and let her be.
She would hang free
inside the chrysalis
that kept her hidden from the world.

So many years have passed.

I am as old as Grandpa was
that spring when I was young.
I live in the house
that once was his.

The garden glows
with cone flowers, purple-blue,
and marigolds,
latana, bright as flame.
And thistles, too.

Now every spring
the Painted Ladies come.
They float and drift like blossoms.
When I walk
they flutter by
to kiss me
with a painted wing.
Sometimes they cling
as though I am a flower myself.

My neighbors cannot understand.
"Our flowers are the same as yours,"
they say each time they visit me.
"We even planted thistles
to invite the butterflies,
but they don't come.
They fill your air
like autumn leaves
although it isn't fall.
It's such a mystery."

I smile.
It's not a mystery at all.

I think my Painted Ladies
talk among themselves
of how their great-great-grandma,
too far back to say,
was saved
from being eaten by a jay.

"This young girl made a house for her,"
they whisper as they fly.
"A painted garden in a box,
so she'd see beauty
as she hung in that half sleep
that we've all known.

"This is the girl,
but older now.
We visit her each spring
to give her back
the love she gave to us
so long ago."

It's not a mystery to me.
I think I know.

How to Raise a Butterfly

1. FINDING A LARVA

An area with brightly colored nectar flowers will attract adult butterflies. Look for the small, wormlike larva on the leaves of plants in the vicinity. Butterfly larvae may be smooth or spiny and are often under two inches in length.

2. PREPARING THE JAR

You will need: a jar without a lid; leaves; a stick about the size of the jar; a piece of tissue paper; tape.

Carry the larva on its leaf. Place it in a jar on top of several more fresh leaves from the same plant on which you found the larva. The leaves will provide nourishment for the larva as it grows into a full-size caterpillar. Place a stick upright in the jar. Using tape, attach tissue paper to cover the jar. The jar should remain stationary, upright, and out of direct sunlight, in an area that is normal room temperature. You will need to collect more leaves as those in the jar dry out or are eaten. It is also very important to clean any droppings out of the jar on a regular basis. After about seven to twelve days in the jar, the caterpillar will climb up and attach itself to the tissue or the stick. AT THIS POINT, IT IS CRUCIAL NOT TO HANDLE OR DISTURB THE JAR. One to two days after the caterpillar has suspended itself, an iridescent chrysalis will appear.

3. BUILDING A BUTTERFLY HOUSE

You will need: a box about one square foot in size; a branch or a stick; plastic wrap or a piece of screen; scissors; tape or glue; paper; crayons or paints (lead-free, not oil-based).

As soon as your caterpillar jar is set up, you will need to build the butterfly house.

Start by placing one end of a stick on the bottom of a box. Lean the other end against the opposite wall. This is very important because the butterfly must be able to hang from a diagonal surface for its wings to dry properly. Next, cut a large window in the side of the box. Attach a sheet of plastic wrap or a screen over the window. On another side of the box, cut a small flap through which to feed the butterfly once it has emerged. When you are not using the flap, keep it taped shut.

Now it's time to paint or color on paper to make backgrounds for the box. Remember to use a lot of green and brown, since these are the colors of a butterfly's natural home. Glue or tape your paintings to the inside of the box when you are done. You can decorate the outside of the box, too.

4. MOVING THE CHRYSALIS TO THE BUTTERFLY HOUSE

Three days after the chrysalis has formed, carefully remove the tissue paper or the stick (whichever the chrysalis is attached to) from the jar, and attach it to the wall of the butterfly house. The chrysalis should hang in the same position as it was in the jar. If it falls off the tissue paper or stick, simply let it lie on the bottom of the box.

Inside the chrysalis, the larva is turning into a butterfly! This will take about seven to ten days.

5. FEEDING THE BUTTERFLY

You will need: the lid of a small jar; a cotton ball or a paper towel; sugar; water.

Make a sugar solution by mixing two teaspoons of sugar with one cup of water. Fill a jar lid with the solution. Make a wick with a piece of cotton or a rolled paper towel and place it in the lid. Be sure the wick is saturated with the solution. The wick should be just long enough to reach about a half inch into the solution, and extend about a half inch above the surface. Set the lid in the box, and be sure to change the sugar solution daily.

Within two to four days after your butterfly has emerged, release the beautiful creature back into nature!